Patience

A Level Three Reader

By Kathryn Kyle

The **Child's World**®

On the cover...
This boy is learning patience. He wants to play outside,
but he must wait until it stops raining.

Published by The Child's World®, Inc.

PO Box 326
Chanhassen, MN 55317-0326
800-599-READ
www.childsworld.com

Special thanks to the Davis, Giroux, Hanzel, Matsuyama, Melaniphy, and Snyder families, and to the staff and students
of Alessandro Volta and Shoesmith Elementary Schools for their help and cooperation in preparing this book.

Photo Credits
© 2003 Claudia Kunin/Stone: 9
© 2003 David Young-Wolff/Stone: cover
© Dennis MacDonald/PhotoEdit: 26
© Flip Schulke/CORBIS: 22
© Hulton-Deutsch Collection/CORBIS: 25
© Romie Flanagan: 3, 5, 6, 10, 13, 14, 17, 18, 21

Project Coordination: Editorial Directions, Inc.
Photo Research: Alice K. Flanagan

Library of Congress Cataloging-in-Publication Data
Kyle, Kathryn.
Patience / by Kathryn Kyle.
    p. cm. — (An Easy reader)
Includes index.
Summary: Easy-to-read scenarios, such as waiting your turn in line or
understanding that your new puppy needs time to learn tricks, provide
lessons in patience.
ISBN 1-56766-090-8 (alk. paper)
1. Patience—Juvenile literature. [1. Patience.]
I. Title. II. Wonder books (Chanhassen, Minn.)
BJ1533.P3 .K95 2002
179'.9—dc21
                          2001007954

What is patience? Patience is waiting your turn or waiting for time to pass. Patience is an important **value**.

At school, you have a question for your teacher. You raise your hand. So do other children in the room. Patience is waiting quietly for the teacher to answer your question.

In the lunch line, you are hungry. The food smells so good! Many people are ahead of you in line. Patience is standing in line and waiting your turn.

On the playground, you are playing in a baseball game. Your team is at bat. Other players have to bat before you. Patience is waiting your turn even when you are excited to play.

At home, you are having a snack with your little sister. She spills her milk on the table. You have to clean it up. Patience is cleaning it up without getting angry. It helps to remember that it was an **accident**.

Tonight your family is going to a movie. You want to leave right away, but your parents are busy. Patience is waiting until everyone is ready to go.

You are on a family vacation. You have a long drive in the car. There is little to do or see. You cannot wait to get to the end of your drive. You want to play! You want to go swimming! Patience is sitting still for a short while longer.

At home, there is a **calendar** on the refrigerator. The date of your birthday is circled on the calendar. You are excited about your birthday. Patience is understanding that many days will pass before your birthday comes.

You finally got a puppy! You have always wanted to have a dog that could do tricks. But this puppy does not know any tricks. Patience is taking the time to teach him tricks.

You are going on a drive to visit
friends. Everything is packed in
the car. You are ready to go. Your
mother forgets something and
has to go back inside. Patience is
waiting for her to return so you
can start the trip.

Many people in history have shown patience. One of these people was Dr. Martin Luther King, Jr. He wanted the people of the United States to change the way they treated African Americans. Dr. King worked hard to make these changes. But things did not change. He kept working. He met with people and gave speeches. His patience made a difference.

← This is a picture of Dr. Martin Luther King, Jr.

Other people watched Dr. King and learned from his patience. Dr. King helped others to be patient. He **encouraged** them to keep working toward their goal. Many of the changes that Dr. King supported did not happen until after his death. Dr. Martin Luther King, Jr. showed patience during his life.

This picture shows Dr. Martin Luther King, Jr. →
giving a speech to thousands of people.

Patience is not always easy. When you really want to do something, patience can be very hard! But patience helps us in our everyday life. How have you shown patience today?

At Home

- Help your brother or sister play a game that they like.

- Wait until your father is off the phone before asking him for help with your homework.

- Let your mother finish her work on the computer before you play a game.

At School

- Take turns reading aloud during story time.

- Wait until the teacher is finished talking before asking a question.

- Sit quietly while the teacher explains something to a classmate.

In Your Community

- Slow down when you are walking with an older neighbor.

- Take turns going down the slide at the park.

- Wait in line quietly with your parents at the grocery store.

Glossary

accident (AK-sih-dent)
An accident is something that happens when you do not expect it. In many accidents, people are hurt or things are broken.

calendar (KAL-en-dur)
A calendar is a chart with all the days of the year.

encouraged (en-KUR-ejd)
To encourage people is to give them support and help them feel good about what they are doing.

value (VAL-yoo)
A value is a person's belief about what is most important in life.

Index

To Find Out More

Books

Bull, Angela. *Free at Last, the Story of Martin Luther King, Jr.* New York: Dorling Kindersley, 1999.

Mattern, Joanne. *Young Martin Luther King, Jr.: "I Have a Dream."* Mawah, N.J.: Troll Communications, 1992.

Walters, Catherine. *When Will It Be Spring?* New York: Dutton, 1998.

White, Rosalyn. *The Magic of Patience: A Jataka Tale.* Berkeley, Calif.: Dharma Publishing, 1990.

Web Sites

BookHugs
http://www.bookhugs.com/sbp.html
To create a story starring you and your friends that highlights patience.

Patience Is a Virtue on the Web
http://www.enchantedlearning.com/Webtipsframe.html#patience
For easy tips about being patient while surfing the Web.

Note to Parents and Educators

Welcome to Wonder Books®! These books provide text at three different levels for beginning readers to practice and strengthen their reading skills. Additionally, the use of nonfiction text provides readers the valuable opportunity to *read to learn*, not just to learn to read.

These leveled readers allow children to choose books at their level of reading confidence and performance. Nonfiction Level One books offer beginning readers simple language, word choice, and sentence structure as well as a word list. Nonfiction Level Two books feature slightly more difficult vocabulary, longer sentences, and longer total text. In the back of each Nonfiction Level Two book are an index and a list of books and Web sites for finding out more information. Nonfiction Level Three books continue to extend word choice and length of text. In the back of each Nonfiction Level Three book are a glossary, an index, and a list of books and Web sites for further research.

State and national standards in reading and language arts emphasize using nonfiction at all levels of reading development. Wonder Books® fill the historical void in nonfiction material for primary grade readers with the additional benefit of a leveled text.

About the Author

Kathryn Kyle has taught elementary school and writes extensively for children. She lives in Minnesota.

DATE DUE

179.9
Kyle

Patience

A.R. 3º - 0.5pt.